PEARLIE OYSTER

HAPPY READING!

This book is especially for:

_____

Suzanne Tate,
Author—
brings fun and
facts to us in her
Nature Series.

James Melvin,
Illustrator—
brings joyous life
to Suzanne Tate's
characters.

Suzanne and James in costume

PEARLIE OYSTER

A Tale of An Amazing Oyster

Suzanne Tate
Illustrated by James Melvin

Nags Head Art
Number 5 of Suzanne Tate's Nature Series

To Regina
a real pearl

Library of Congress Catalog Card Number 89-92226
ISBN 0-9616344-7-2
Published by
Nags Head Art, Inc., P.O. Drawer 1809, Nags Head, NC 27959
Copyright © 1989 by Suzanne Tate

Pearlie Oyster was a Common Oyster.

Her house was made of two shells.

The shells were gray and rough
and ugly on the outside.

But Pearlie's shell was pretty on the inside!
She was smooth and pink and pearlie white.

Pearlie began life as a tiny animal.
She floated in the water
and ate tiny plants drifting there.

In a very short time, she had two little shells.

When Pearlie was only two weeks old,
she settled to the bottom of the water.
She attached herself to a log.

Pearlie was not lonesome there.
Other oysters were on the log, too.
They were called a "bed" of oysters.

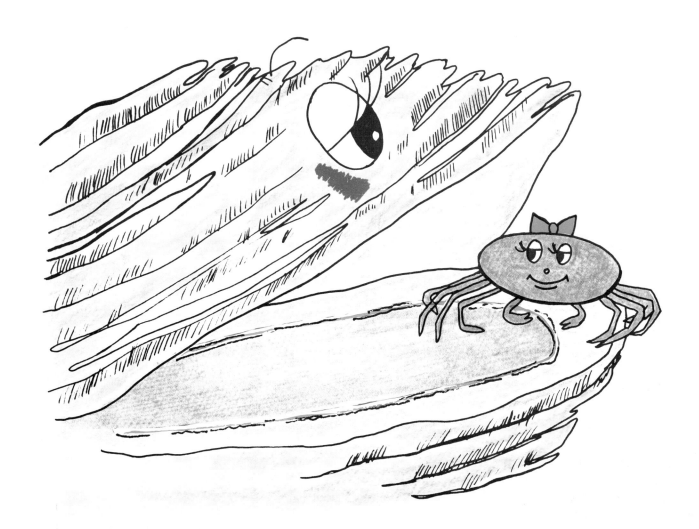

One day when Pearlie was still young,
a tiny crab crawled into her shell.
The tiny crab was Miss Patty Pea Crab.

She stayed inside Pearlie's shell
all of the time.
Whenever Pearlie opened her mouth to feed,
Miss Patty ate the leftovers.

"How are you doing?" Miss Patty said
to Pearlie one morning.
"Not so good," replied Pearlie.
"I have this terrible ITCH."

"How did you get that?" asked Miss Patty.
"Last night when I was feeding,
a grain of sand floated into my mouth.
Now I can't get rid of it," said Pearlie.

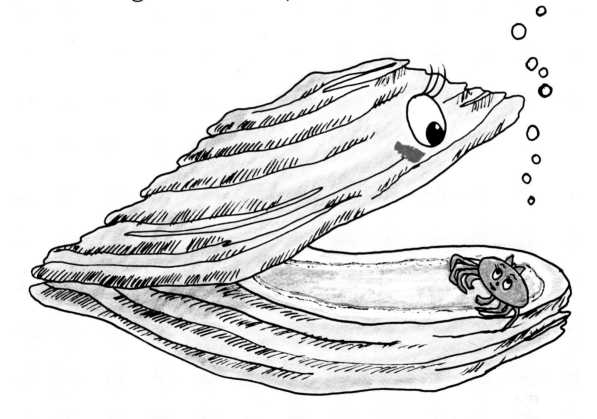

"I heard that a grain of sand in oysters
becomes something beautiful," said Miss Patty.

"I don't believe that," said Pearlie.

"You have to have faith," replied Miss Patty.

"Well, I don't believe in anything
I can't see," said Pearlie.

"It's just a bad ITCH to me."

Pearlie tried to forget her ITCH.

She opened up her mouth to feed.

Even though she stayed in one place,

there was plenty of food.

One day Petey Pea Crab came along.
He was Miss Patty's boyfriend.
When Pearlie opened her mouth to feed,
he would sneak right in!

Petey Pea Crab was much smaller
than Miss Patty.
He didn't try to stay inside Pearlie.
He just came to visit.

"Your boyfriend is a little feller,"
Pearlie said to Miss Patty.
"Aren't you robbing the cradle?"
"Oh, he's the same age as I,"
replied Miss Patty. "He's just little.
But we get along like two peas in a pod."

Now the grain of sand was getting
bigger and bigger.
Pearlie had been covering it with juice inside her shell.
(It helped the ITCH.)

Miss Patty could see something
shiny and white and beautiful.

That grain of sand had become a pearl!

Pearlie could hardly believe it.
Something good had come
out of something bad!

Miss Patty Pea Crab was excited.
"You see how pretty that grain of sand
is now," she said.
Let's have a party to show it off!"

Pearlie agreed.

The news went fast through the oyster bed.

Pearlie would show off
a brand new pearl!

She opened up her shell
so the other oysters could see the pearl.

And they opened up their mouths
in amazement!

"Oh, how pretty your pearl is, Pearlie,"
they all said.
"You are amazing!"

Pearlie thanked them politely.
"Just think, I first took that ITCH
with a grain of sand, and now it
is a beautiful pearl."

Then she said to Miss Patty,
"I am going to give you the pearl
for a wedding gift."

Miss Patty was so excited
that she jumped up and down!
It tickled Pearlie.

"It's been an exciting day," Pearlie said.
She closed up her shell
and settled down on the log to rest.
"Now it is time to go to bed!"